Over the Hills

Hills

Brie Kraus

The characters and events portrayed in this book are fictitious. Any similarity to real persons, living or dead, is coincidental and not intended by the author. To the extent any real names of individuals, locations, or organizations are included in the book, they are used fictitiously and not intended to be taken otherwise.

To all who love a good mystery.

Over the
Hills

Chapter 1

June, 1974

The Glow family were similar to any typical family living on a rough council estate in the city of Manchester. They were unemployed, had little money and overall, were experiencing an economic depression. During this time, many people turned to alcohol, and nobody cared about anybody else ,but themselves and their own families. Times were hard, and many did not see a way out of it. Nobody knew if they were ever going to experience happiness again. The country was in such a terrible state at this time, and that was that.

Ian Glow was like any other child going through these times: eight years of age, and often had little to eat outside of school hours and loved to make people laugh. He had no idea of the situation the country was in, as he was too young to understand, and was too occupied with his own childhood to even try to. He had grown up in one house on a council estate, as did his elder sister (Hannah, 17) and brother (Ernest, 6).

Ernest was known as a geek. In typical nerd fashion, wore square glasses, and had two teeth at the front of his mouth that stuck out. He was always in the background, a perfect target for bullies, and Ian could not do anything but sit back and watch, as he was powerless against them. Ernest did not fit in at all with the rest of the family; he was too intelligent, though none of the other members of the family seemed to notice.

Hannah, on the other hand, was a typical teenage girl, beautiful, loved talking with her friends and checking out boys, spending most of her time going out and dressing her hair.

The night of 1984, started out like any other, quiet outside and with nobody around, nobody except the entire Glow family, excluding the one who did not bother to speak to any of them.

"Bitch, I asked for a steak pie, not a pork one!" cried Trevor, the patriarch of the family.

"Do I care?" asked Iris, the matriarch, drinking a large glass of wine

"You will in a moment if you don't keep your trap shut!" screamed an enraged Trevor.

The entire family watched on the sides of the living room, knowing what was about to happen next. Iris' parents, Margaret and Fred, who lived next door to the family, watched as well, not caring much, despite the fact that all three children were there. The two boys watched in fear, while Hannah paid little attention. She was too busy putting on some make-up for her night out. Iris' sister, Alison, was also there, though she and Iris did not get along.

"Here they go again!" laughed Margaret.

Fred laughed with her.

"And if you don't shut up I'll ram your head into that door!" yelled Trevor.

"Don't talk to her like that!" Iris cried, getting up to attack Trevor, but all she managed was a wobble since she drunk, as usual. The rest of the family had no idea where she got the alcohol from. Maybe there was a secret supplier, they thought.

Iris half-limped over to Trevor, and as she tried to hit him, but Trevor jumped out of the way, turned on her, and punched her three times in the mouth; two of her teeth fell out, and her face turned red. She screamed for him to stop, but he didn't listen, and neither did anybody else. She didn't cared anymore.

"You go girl!" cried Iris' father, enjoying the action.

Iris picked up a knife and cut into Trevor's hand.

"I'm gonna kill you!" he cried.

Iris tried to run away, but he seized her hair and yanked it. She screamed for somebody to help her.

Suddenly, out of nowhere, Ian jumped up, and ran to them, trying, in vain, to stop the frequent abuses of his father, no longer able to bear watching them.

"Let go of her now!" Ian cried.

Bewildered. Trevor let go of his wife.

"What did you just say?" he said, in complete shock.

"I hate you! I'm gonna tell the police!"

Trevor grabbed hold of little Ian and smacked his head against the wall and punched Ian in the stomach. Poor little Ernest screamed in fear, but Hannah laughed, crying, "Go on, dad! Kick the shit out of him!"

When Trevor had finished, Ian collapsed to the floor, covered in his own blood.

"And don't you ever, ever stand up to me again!" Trevor screamed, kicking Ian once more.

Alison, who still remained next to her parents—who acted as though they watching a television program—decided that enough was enough.

"Right, I'd best be off," she said, her voice trembling.

"See ya, love!" said Margaret, kissing her on the hand.

Alison left, telling herself that she had not witnessed any of what she had just seen.

Hannah then got up. "Right, I'm ready," she said.

"And where are you going?" Trevor asked.

"I'm going to my friend's party," she replied. "Isn't it obvious? I'm wearing a pink dress!"

"Well go on then," said Trevor.

Hannah left, while Ernest hid under a table and Ian lay crumpled on the floor in agony. Iris continued drinking her liquor, and Trevor sat down to finish his pork pie.

Outside, in the cold, early hours of morning, a person remained out in the middle of a field, digging. In the freshly dug hole, the mysterious person placed a body, a female body, inside. As dirt flew through the air, covering the hole, remnants of a pink dress poked out.

Chapter 2

It was one week after the Hartfield murders case, but I was still receiving vast amounts of media attention, although there was now little attention left to receive. To me, it was in the past, and I focused all of my energy into the next murder case that I was assigned to, even if it meant going back to the gang killings.

"Has everything settled down now?" asked Miranda, my colleague and sometime friend.

I thought that Miranda was a bit jealous of my achievement, since she never used that sort of deduction power in her life. If she had been assigned to the Hartfield case, the murderer would have gotten away and an innocent person would have been sent to prison. Although I was proud of my accomplishment, I did not brag about it.

To my bewilderment, there was still a newspaper article about me pinned up on the boss' wall when I entered the room, even though seven days had gone by. I was very pleased that Clive Mitchell had thought so much about me; that was something else for Miranda to be jealous of.

"Well, to be honest, Miranda," I'm glad the whole thing is over with," I replied to her, before I went into the boss' office, ready to be assigned to my next case. I assumed it was another gang killing, because that was what they generally were; the gang violence in Manchester was at its highest rate in 2012, which tired me sometimes. However, I should have known better than to make assumptions.

"Williams," he begun, as I entered the room, "I have a new case for you, and I think you'll like it."

"Alright," I replied, waiting for more information, and eager to discover what the man had in store for me. Inside, I was honest with myself, that not much could be trickier than solving the Hartfield murders, but I knew that I could be surprised.

"Well," said Mitchell, "this morning, we, or should I say, a dog, found a body of an unidentified victim. There is not much left but bones, and they appear to be a female. I'll let you look at it, and you'll see the rest. I've chosen you for this case because I trust you. I have faith that you will solve this cold case. You have already demonstrated your amazing skills to me, so this should be no problem to you."

Mitchell's assumption annoyed me. Sometimes, murders are unsolvable, especially cold cases, since there are no leads from the start. It's sad, but unfortunately, Mitchell did not see it like that. He saw me as the God of criminal catching, and I knew that I wasn't.

Although I was talented at what I did, I could not make any conclusions about a case if I did not have anything to deduce from, and this case seemed just like that. On the other hand, it was worth a shot, and it was better than working on gang killings, and, I was ready for the challenge.

I arrived at the crime scene: an empty field in the middle of nowhere—the perfect place to dump a body. There were no houses, and no public facilities. It was just an empty field. A few hundred feet away, in the distance, I could see several small hills which were clumped together, but that was literally all there was to see. No roads were to be found; the field was connected to other abandoned fields, allowing the local forest to be seen.

I approached the forensics team, knowing that the remains would still be there, what was left them, anyway, which consisted of bone fragments, a femur, and a skull. Something caught my eye. Attached to one of the bones was a fragment of cotton material: it was pink.

"Have you got any DNA on this person?" I asked a forensic scientist.

"Unfortunately, we've looked around the area, and there are no fingerprints on the victim's dress, and obviously, any fingerprints that would have been on the victim are gone now. There are no hairs on the body, aside from her own, so no, there is no DNA evidence, thus far, I'm afraid," he replied.

That was a huge drawback for me. DNA was the easy way out, but it looked as though to me that this case was going to be a tough one.

"Do you know how the victim was killed?" I asked the forensic scientist.

"The scratch marks on the bones suggest that the victim was stabbed at least nine times," he replied, "but I will need to examine them more closely to know for sure."

Inside, I felt sick. How could somebody do this to another human being?

I took another look at the bones, imagining the pain the girl must have suffered before she died.

"There's no teeth!" I cried.

"Yes. That's one of the most horrific parts. The person who did this probably pulled this woman's teeth out, from what I can tell by looking at the mouth," replied the forensic scientist.

I thought I was going to throw up. Why would somebody do that? Perhaps it was to make sure that the body was not identified. That was the only explanation I could think of right now. Other than that, torture. Now that the victim had no teeth, I could not even compare the victim's teeth with any dental records. This was going to be a very hard case for me, but I felt a strong connection with the victim, for some reason. I made it my new personal goal to make sure that the person who did this would be caught, dead or alive.

Chapter 3

My first step was to conduct some door to door research around the area, to see if anybody knew anything about this mysterious, unidentified woman. I hoped, and prayed, that there would be somebody old enough to remember the disappearance of a woman in the area. I was not completely certain that the dumping ground was in fact anywhere near to the place where this woman lived, but the killer must have known the area well, or else they would not be able to find this place, since it was in the middle of nowhere, and it would be virtually impossible to discover by accident, especially with a body in the trunk. This murder was planned; that I was sure of. Somebody wanted this woman dead.

I started with the door to door inquiries, but, to my great misfortune, nobody knew a thing about it. For years, people had been walking their dogs through this field, ignorant of the fact that they walked over the top of a corpse. It was a shame that nobody had tried to regenerate the field, because if a farmer had found her years before, we would have had perhaps half a chance of identifying this woman. Since the door to door inquiries did little good, I decided to return to the station, to wait for the post mortem.

Later that day, the post mortem came back revealed that the woman probably died somewhere between the years of 1980 and 1990. That was useful to an extent, because if I were to find a lead, I could relate back to this to help identify the woman. However, it did not help me get any closer to identifying the woman at the moment, which was the most important thing. All I needed was one person to come forward and say that they knew this mystery woman. Somebody did. I was certain of it. Somebody had to know details about this woman's disappearance. The report also said that she was probably between the ages of twenty and thirty-five. That narrowed it down slightly, but it still did not help much. I was going to go to the missing person's database to see if I could get a lead on this, but I asked Mitchell (not the boss, the other Mitchell) to go instead, as I was too busy analysing the report.

The report also contained the grisly details of the woman's death; where on the body she was stabbed, how deep the wounds were, what type of instrument was used, and so on. It proved to be of little use, even though I now knew exactly how she died. I had previously deduced that the person who killed her was a psychopath, though a very clever one, as they had got away with it, up until now, at least. I hoped that this person was still alive so that they could get punished for what they had done. Nobody deserved to die that way.

Mitchell returned with several flies, full of details of women between the ages of twenty and thirty-five who went missing between the years of 1980 and 1990 in England. Finally, things were narrowed down a bit, as there were only thirteen reported missing people. For the first time, I began to get quite excited, since I now had pictures of people and different pieces of information to go on.

Sadly, none of the files gave any details about a woman in a pink dress—some had been out on parties the night they vanished, and others were at home, so I was able to narrow things down even further, but I still had seven women who were on the suspect list. I was close, but sadly, not close enough, as I could not come up with a convincing argument, with evidence, that any of the women in the files were actually the dead woman found earlier today. I assumed that most of these women were dead themselves, but I knew deep down that one of these women was the woman we had found. Although it was possible that the woman was not reported missing, it was improbable, as there was likely to be somebody who noticed her disappearance and reported her.

Seeing nowhere else to go, I decided to launch a public appeal in order to see if anybody knew this woman. This was probably, and hopefully, going to be the most challenging part of the case. The television and radio companies stormed in with this story, eager to report the discovery of this mystery woman. They gave details of where she had been found, and the pink dress that she wore. I hoped that somebody would be able to recall the pink dress, even though there was no mention of it in any of the missing person's files, so I knew that it was a long shot, but worth a try, as I had nothing at all to lose.

I was extremely lucky, because the very next day, a visitor arrived at the station, wanting to talk to me about the missing woman.

"Hello," I said to her, as she walked in.

She was a small woman, aged around fifty, and she wore clothes that came from a thrift shop, matching her greasy hair and speckled face, which accentuated her plump figure.

"My name is Lesley Kicks," she said, quite nervous to talk to me.

"I'm Tammy Williams," I said, eager to see what this woman knew, "I understand that you have some information about the woman we found?"

"Yes," Lesley replied, taking a seat, "and I think it might be very useful to you."

"Go on," I said.

"Well, I think the missing woman was Yvonne Lennox, if you don't know that already."

I remembered the name from one of the missing person's files. She had gone out for a party that night, but the person who reported her could not recall what she was wearing.

"And why do you think that?" I asked Lesley.

"Because she was wearing the pink dress the night she went missing. I remember it. I am...was a very good friend of Yvonne, and when she went missing I knew that she'd been murdered. It was just so unusual of her," Lesley replied in a shaky voice.

I began to get very excited now.

"And why did you not say any of this before?" I asked her.

"Because one of my other friends said she sorted it out. She said she told the police everything and that there was no need to speak to them. I've only just realized that she never mentioned the dress. I know it's Yvonne. It has to be," replied Lesley, getting excited.

"Right, and can you tell me about the time she went missing?" I asked her.

"I can't really remember," she said.

"Can you remember the last time you saw her?"

"Well, we were at the party just a few miles away from here, in a club. A lot of people were quite drunk. Yvonne went out for a cigarette, and that was that. She never came back in."

Lesley started to cry.

"It's OK," I said, reassuring her.

I thanked her for the help she gave me, and gave her the contact details should she ever think of anything else. I now had the name of the victim, because Yvonne went missing in 1988, and she was twenty-eight years old. In a way, come to think of it, she looked quite a lot like the skeleton. I now had the name of the victim, and I prepared for the rest of the journey ahead.

Chapter 4

My first task was to find out if any of Yvonne Lennox' relatives were alive, other than her friends. I telephoned Lesley again, informed her that the body we had found was indeed Yvonne's, and asked her if Yvonne had any living relatives. Lesley told me that Yvonne had a sister, Evelyn, who was now quite old. She gave me her contact details, and I went out to find her.

When I first met Evelyn, I noticed that she still looked upset. She must have been told the news, I thought to myself. This was confirmed when she opened the door to allow us inside, as she said to us, "I have been waiting for this news for twenty-four years."

She picked up a handkerchief from her pocket and wiped her eye clean. I knew that she had felt like it was a giant weight lifted off her shoulders. However, justice was not yet served, so although Evelyn knew what happened to her sister, and how she died, the killer was not yet found, and that was my main purpose for coming to see her.

Previously, I had done some research about Yvonne, and discovered that she had divorced and filed an official complaint about him, that he had assaulted her on several occasions. However, before any further action could be taken, Yvonne was killed. This made me very suspicious of her ex-husband, Keith Lennox.

"Mrs. Dutchie," I asked Evelyn, "I know this is hard for you, but I need to talk to you about Evelyn."

"Of course," said Evelyn, gathering herself together, "come inside, please."

She invited Graham Mitchell and I inside, and we sat down with her. I decided that I needed to get this out the way for her as quickly as possible, so I asked the questions straight away.

"We need to establish when you last saw Yvonne, if you can remember," I asked the poor old woman.

"Of course I can remember," replied Evelyn, "it was the day she went missing, or died, as we know now. God, I still can't get over it. Deep down, I knew that she was dead, but I had hoped it was a quick and painless death, not one like this. Who can do such a thing?" she asked.

"In time, you will find the answer to that," I replied, trying to reassure her, "but for now, we need to establish a few basic facts about Yvonne's life, particularly on the day she went missing. Can you tell us if she made any unusual calls, or if she was behaving strangely?"

"No, that's the thing! She was behaving normally. I just don't understand," Evelyn replied.

"Did Yvonne have any enemies?"

"Well, there was the obvious one," said Evelyn, "her husband was the horrible one. He hit her a few times, you know?"

"We've read the files about that," I said, trying not to get into any details about it, "but do you really think he was capable of killing her?"

"Well, it's been decades since I saw him last. I saw him just before the divorce; I don't know where he is now, but he was a very aggressive man, and it was his way or no way. That's what it was like around him."

"OK," I said, "and is there anyone else who hated Yvonne?"

"I don't think so. Not with a passion, anyway."

I decided to leave things there.

"There is one more thing," said Evelyn.

I was intrigued.

"Go on," I said to her, Mitchell ready with his notepad.

"Well, I think Keith was stalking Yvonne."

"Why do you think that?" I asked her, rather interested by this revelation.

"Yvonne carried pepper spray. And another thing: a few days before Yvonne died, she was on the telephone with Keith. I was at her house, and she mentioned his name a few times."

"What did she say to him?" I asked, somehow thinking that this piece of information could be important.

"Well, I remember a bit of it that's stuck with me for the rest of my life. Yvonne said to Keith, 'I know it's you. I know it's you who is standing at my window all the time'."

"Did you asked her about it?" I asked, intrigued.

"I tried to, but she changed the subject. I tried to help her, I really did, but now I realize if I had help her, maybe she wouldn't have died!"

Evelyn broke down into tears, I sat her down, calmed her down and left.

The next thing we had to do was to trace Keith Lennox. He was around somewhere; I knew it. I knew that at this point in the case, it was probable that he was the murderer.

We found him. He lived the next town over. We approached him, as he stood, talking to someone in the middle of the street. We were able to trace him easily because we went to his flat first, and a neighbour had told us that he had gone downtown. I was prepared for a chase.

Just as we expected, as we approached him, he said, "I've done nothing wrong."

"We'd like you to answer a few questions down at the station, if you don't mind," said Mitchell.

He ran off. He was a fast and it took about three minutes for us to catch him, and twice as long to escort him back to the car.

We entered the interview room later that day. He folded his arms and he glared at us.

"Do you remember a woman called Yvonne Lennox?" I asked him.

"What do you think?" said Keith, trying to be clever with us.

"Well, she was your wife. Now, your divorced. Can you tell us why that is?"

He looked at us for a few seconds, remaining quiet, and then he said to us, "Well, you're the police officer. You work it all out."

"Believe me, I will," I said, "and if you don't start talking now we'll charge you with murder."

"Who the Hell has been murdered?" he said, trying to look confused.

"Your ex-wife," Mitchell told him.

"Which one?" asked Keith.

Mitchell and I glanced at each other.

"Yvonne Lennox was killed almost twenty-five years ago," I replied, "do you remember her disappearance?"

"No," Keith replied.

"Well, she was murdered shortly after your divorce, and before she died, she was about to go to court because she claimed that you were domestically abusing her."

"I don't know nothing," he said, folding his arms.

"Also, Yvonne claimed that you were stalking her."

"No comment," said Keith.

Unfortunately, as we continued to question him, he kept saying, "No comment." Although usually, that was a sign that the person was guilty of a crime, I thought that Keith was too lazy to speak to us anymore. So, we looked into his criminal history, and he was clean. I couldn't believe it. We had to release him without charge. I was devastated, but before he left, I warned him that I would be keeping a close eye on him.

However, I had something else to be shocked about. In a surprise twist to the investigation, I received a call from the boss.

"Are you sitting down?" DI Mitchell asked me.

"I am now," I replied. "Why?"

"Because you're about to be in shock. At the field where Yvonne Lennox was found, we've discovered another seven corpses."

Chapter 5

It took us five days to identify each individual murder victim, but we got there in the end. It was difficult, because like Yvonne Lennox, each victim had had their teeth pulled out. I was certainly not expecting this to happen; I was dealing with a complete, utter psychopath.

The first victim of the extra second we identified was Irene Dunneford. She was forty-eight years of age when she went missing in 1990. She was a nurse, the mother of two children, and lived around the Hartfield area. On the day she went missing, the last person to have seen her was her husband.

She said that she was going out, but no CCTV evidence confirmed that she had ever made it to town. Some suspected that she had taken a shortcut home, and that was that for her. I would look into more detail about this later. As far as the forensics could make out, she was beaten to death with something metallic, especially across the skull, but also the spine.

The second victim was named John Christie, aged forty-nine, when he went missing in 1990. He worked in a petrol station and lived just outside of town. He had a wife and son; his wife was long gone, but his son was still alive. It was his wife who had last seen him. He said goodbye to her before going to work, but he never made it. His family knew that he had been murdered, and they had launched several search parties over the years for him to be found. He was shot in the head, but also suffered two shots to the chest from a shotgun.

The third victim was Sienna Stewart. She was aged thirty-seven. Although she had no family, she had many friends and was a very sociable person, so it was unusual for her not to make any contact with anybody for several days. She was murdered in 1989, apparently by electric shocks to the skull. The forensics thought that she may have been subjected to torture by some sort of powerful source of electricity before her death. The last time she was seen, or heard from, was a phone call to her mother, who was dead by the time her body was found.

The fourth victim was the most shocking, and that was that of a fourteen year old boy, whose name was Kieran Bradley. He was an aspiring Olympic cyclist, and he had many friends in the school where he lived. He was killed in 1988, just after Yvonne Lennox went missing as well. He was choked to death; forensic scientists found that several dozen cotton wool balls had been forced down his throat. He was a very popular child at school. I thought it was horrific when I told his parents about the discovery, and how he had died. I will never forget their faces.

The fifth victim was an elderly lady, named Elizabeth Beckett, eighty-three; an old age pensioner, with three children, and eight grandchildren. Over her life, she had been an influential woman, as she had taught for forty years. She came to a grisly end when her limbs had been chopped off. Forensics identified the murder weapon as an axe; somebody had chopped her legs off and left her to bleed to death before she was buried, and this was in 1991.

The sixth victim was Fred Aylesbury, seventy-eight, and he was considered a respectable member of the community. He had been a football coach and a youth worker for most of his life. He was married, with five children and fifteen grandchildren. He was the only victim to have been found in a box, killed in 1994, and the killer simply placed him in a box while tied up, cut his teeth out, nailed the box shut and buried him, leaving him to suffocate.

Finally, the body of a twenty-two year old man was found. He went missing in 1996, and his name was Christopher Eggles, and he was a student training to be a surgeon. He had a very promising career ahead of him, girlfriend, and they were even considering getting married and starting a family. He was last seen leaving the university. His car was found in Hartfield forest, which was a few miles away from where his body had been discovered. The car had crashed into a tree, but there was no trace of him. He had been choked to death, probably by a rope. The forensic scientists were not completely sure, but they thought that he had been tied up and hung from a tree nearby.

After having finished reading the files on each victim, I sat back for a moment. Was this really happening? How could anybody in the world do this to a fellow human being? I almost cried, but I knew that I needed to get my head together and focus on the case, leaving my emotions to one side. After all, it was what solved the case last time for me, but I knew that this case would be a tough one, as no DNA evidence had been left anywhere on the scene, so I was dealing with a somewhat intelligent person, no matter how twisted, or psychotic, they were.

I started looking for connections between the victims, if any. I knew from the start that each victim was completely different. They were in a variety of ages, and their personalities and jobs were all different. Even the way they all died differed (apart from choking and strangulation, which were quite similar, and excluding the fact that they all had their teeth pulled out). They all lived in other sections of Manchester, and they all lead different lives, so how could it be possible that the killer could be acquainted with each of them? What did all of these people have in common? It was going to be tough, so I decided to sleep on it, if I could.

Chapter 6

I woke up the next morning, not knowing where to go, or what to do next. I slept little, as I had lain awake for several hours in bed, thinking about the murderer and who it could be, like I always did. I tried to create a profile in my mind of this psychopath: probably male, had a very disturbed past, and was reasonably intelligent. I could not think of anything else. What possible motive could there be for murdering these innocent people? Perhaps there was no motive; perhaps they were driven and motivated by their excitement of killing a human being.

I arrived at the station, and Patricia approached me.

"Tammy, there is someone here who wants to speak to you," she said, pointing to a woman who looked like she was in her fifties.

I walked over to the woman, and it was clear to me that it was a relative of one of the victims. Her eyes were red from having received some devastating news, although she probably knew it already, deep down.

"Hello," I said, approaching her as kindly and as friendly as I possibly could.

"Are you the one who is working on the Kieran Bradley case?" she asked.

It suddenly hit me. She must have been Kieran Bradley's mother, the one who was killed when he was fourteen.

"I am," I replied, trying not to show my emotions too much.

"Well, I need to talk to you about something," she said.

"Take your time," I told her, allowing her to sit down and talk to me somewhere private, in the soft interview room.

"So, what is it you want to talk to me about?" I asked her, after offering her some coffee. She had refused, as she just wanted to get this conversation over with.

"I might have a little bit of information to give you about the murders," she said. "There were eight more, weren't there?" she asked.

"There were eight in total," I replied.

After hearing that, she gasped, and her hand ran down her fragile face. She was bewildered at the fact that her son had died at the hands of a psychotic serial killer.

"Were they all young boys?" was her next question.

"No," was my straight answer, "there were also some women, and each victim was of different ages.

Some were old, some were young, and others were middle-aged."

"So why did he pick my son?" she said, trying not to shout too loud.

"I'm trying my best to get to the bottom of that, I really am, but for now, I need as much information as I possibly can," I replied, trying to keep the poor woman as calm as possible.

"That's why I'm here," she said, "I've got an idea about who the killer might be."

"Go on," I urged.

"Well, the killer might, just might, be Ian Glow."

"Who is he?"

"He's that strange man who used to live near us. I don't know where he lives now."

"And why do you think he's the killer?"

"Well, I remembered back to when I had a conversation with my son. It was one of the last conversations I had.

"It was a normal day, and I was dropping Kieran off at school in the car. Before he left, he talked to me about Ian Glow. He pointed him out. At that point, Ian was talking to some young children. He must have been in his twenties back then! Anyway, Kieran started saying things about him.

"'That's the one who talks about killing people all of the time', he told me.

'That one who is talking to the kids right now?' I asked him.

"'Yeah. He's always talking about how he would want to die, and if he were to kill someone, he would torture them and bury them alive'.

"'Well, there is clearly something seriously wrong with that man. Why does he come here? He looks too old to go to school!'

"'The teachers have shooed him away a few times, but he keeps coming back'.

"'Why?'

"'I don't know. Nobody really talks to him. I suppose he just likes it here'.

"Kieran then got out of the car, and as he went into school; Ian turned around and watched him enter. As the door closed, he went back to his conversation."

I was writing notes down at this point. I had finally gotten a new lead.

"Why didn't you come forward about this before?" I asked her.

"Because I forgot all about it. I was more concerned about Kieran's welfare. At least, I know now, and the forensics, or somebody, told me that there was no sign of sexual abuse, so at least he didn't die that way, even if he was..."

She broke down.

"It OK," she said.

I allowed her to leave, and told her that I would keep her updated.

To my utter astonishment, ten minutes later, a police officer arrived in the station with a man in handcuffs.

"This is Ian Glow," said the police officer, "and I've caught him hanging around the field where the bodies were found. I just thought you'd be interested."

Chapter 7

The policeman was right: I was, in fact, very interested, in what this man had to say. I had no idea who he was, but I wanted to know why he went to the field where the bodies were found. Perhaps he knew something about the murders? Or perhaps, he was even the killer himself, but I knew I was getting too excited for that, but then again, why go there when the field is in the middle of nowhere? He had obviously seen it on the news, that eight corpses had been found in a field in Manchester, so he must have known.

The man himself, Ian Glow, looked like he was in his forties, although he did have grey hair and was very scruffy looking. He had a short beard, and it was clear to me that he had not had a wash for several days. He was obviously quite a poor person, probably from the council estate. From what Mrs. Bradley told me, this man was undoubtedly insane, and he looked at me with a guilty face. He seemed to be depressed. I wondered if he was the same horror and death fanatic as he used to be. There was only one way to find out.

"Would you like to follow me into the interview room?" I asked him, escorting him there.

"I need my tablets at dinner time," he said.

"What?" I asked him.

"I need my anti-depressants."

I looked at the clock. It was after twelve now, so I assumed that he was late in taking his tablets.

"Alright, Ian," I said, "I'll get somebody to go and get your tablets, so you need to tell me where you live."

Nervous, Ian told me his address. I knew he had something to hide; there was something in that house that made me worried. I hoped and prayed that there would not be any more dead bodies in there. I asked Graham and Miranda to go along to the house, since they had nothing better to do.

Meanwhile, I interviewed Ian Glow, hoping that this would be a real lead into the case, as I was more determined than ever to apprehend the person responsible for these ghastly crimes.

"So, Ian," I begun, "do you mind telling me why you went to the field that day?"

There was no answer. I tried asking again. He breathed, as if he was about to say something, but he did not.

"There must be a reason why you went there," I asked him.

"I'm not up for talking right now," he said, talking to me with his face to the floor.

"OK," I replied, trying to be nice to him, "I'll get you some coffee or something, and then we can talk?"

"I would like to have my tablets," he said.

It took fifteen minutes for Graham and Miranda to return to the police station with the tablets. While Miranda handed Ian the pills, Graham took me to one side.

"You didn't find anything then?" I asked him.

"We didn't find any dead bodies," Graham replied, "but it is not good."

"What's in there?" I asked him, desperate to hear the answer as the suspense was killing me.

"We went into his bedroom where the tablets were," he said, "and we found these strange drawings on the wall."

"What was on these drawings?"

"There were dead bodies, people who'd been tortured, and people who'd been murdered."

"Good God!" I cried, "we are dealing with a psychopath!"

"No, I'm afraid you are," replied Graham, carrying on with his work.

I returned to the interview room, wondering what was going through this man's mind. Ian had taken the tablets, and so he was ready to talk—the drugs had worked.

"So, Ian," I said, starting over, "can you now tell me why you were hanging around in the field?"

"I will now," he said, "it's because I was told to go there."

"By who?" I said, thinking that he was lying.

"I received a phone call. It was a man. He told me to go to the field."

"And when did you receive this phone call?" I asked him, knowing that I could check the phone records later.

"I don't know the exact time."

"Did this person say who it was?"

"No, they just said, 'go to the field tomorrow morning', and they put the phone down."

"Did you not think to tell the police?"

"No," was the simple answer he gave me.

I tired of the interview already, so I decided to move on to something else.

"Do you like the idea of killing people?" I asked Ian.

No answer.

"I know the answer to that, Ian," I said, "because two of my colleagues have already been to your house, and they have found these unusual, sadistic drawings."

"That doesn't make me a killer," he said.

What he just said intrigued me very much.

"Why did you just say that?" I asked him, not knowing the response.

"Because I know you think I did it!" he yelled, getting up as if to attack me.

"Calm down now!" I said, raising my voice as well.

"I'm telling you I am not the killer! I did not kill those people!"

"Did you watch the news the other day?" I asked him.

Ian nodded, his face facing the floor again before sitting down, and looking depressed. I decided to talk to him about his family.

"What was your upbringing like?" I asked him.

"My upbringing?"

"Yes. What were your parents like? Did you have any grandparents, or brothers or sisters?"

"I had all of those," Ian replied, still not looking at me.

"What were they like?"

Ian looked at me for a second, and then decided to open up.

"My father used to beat me, he replied, and my mother was an alcoholic. Some days, I would go hungry, and the only food I often received in a day was at school, or if I was lucky enough to find some money somewhere to go to a shop. They treated my little brother, Ernest, the same."

I was not expecting that reply at all, but there was more.

"My grandparents used to sit and laugh while my father beat me up almost every day. Ernest used to be so scared that he hid under the table. My sister used to laugh at me as well. She went out most of the time. She must have been brought up that way too. And then there was my aunt. She was the most caring out of the lot, but did nothing to stop them—she just blocked it out of her life."

"Were there any other family members?" I asked.

"There was Nathan, who was my mother's brother. He left when I was a baby, and never spoke to us again. I remember, when we were teenagers, Ernest telephoned him, but he just put the phone down. I suppose he was treated the same way as the rest of us."

Ian stopped talking, leaving me to think. Who on Earth were these people? I knew I had to put my emotions to one side, and focus on the case.

"Right, Ian," I said to him, "I am going to arrest you for the murders. You will be looked after in the cells."

"You're wrong!" he cried. "I did not kill those people! I'm innocent!"

I knew that was what they all said, but that did not matter. I knew that there was a small chance that Ian Glow was not the killer, but it was very unlikely.

However, I noticed something, and I did a little more research and found out something very intriguing. I looked for photographs of each of the family members, and compared them with photographs of the victims. It was then when it hit me. I noticed that each family member had an astonishing resemblance to one of the victims. For example, Yvonne Lennox strongly resembled Hannah Glow, Ian's sister. I knew then that I probably had the killer, but I knew that further research was to be done in order to convince a jury.

Chapter 8

I sat back and thought for a moment: Ian Glow.
Was that the name of a psychotic serial killer? Was he
even the killer at all, or was this whole thing a red
herring and therefore a waste of valuable time? I was
determined to get to the bottom of this, no matter
what, and although it looked as though I was coming
to the end of the case already, it did not feel like it. In
the other cases I had solved, whenever I was close to
solving it, I felt something inside. I just had this
sensation that I was right, but I just did not feel it for
this one. Perhaps it was because the case was far too
depressing, more twisted than any other case I'd been
involved with, but I knew the job had to be done, since
justice was on the line, and lots of it.

First of all, I decided to research Ian Glow's
relatives. In the interview, he had mentioned his
parents, his grandparents, an aunt, an uncle (although
he was never in his life) a brother, and a sister. That
totaled eight people: the same number of victims there

were in the field. My theory for now was that Ian Glow had imagined killing his abusive family whilst killing these innocent victims. Perhaps that was his way of releasing his anger. He would have wanted to kill his parents because of the abuse, his grandparents because they supported the abuse, his aunt because she turned a blind eye, his sister because she did not care, and his uncle because he knew about the abuse, yet he did nothing about it. However, there was still one big question that stood out: why would he want to kill his little brother? What did he ever do? I wanted to find out, but first, I needed to know more about the family, and if there were any still alive.

It was most likely that Ernest, the brother, or Hannah, the sister, would still be living, and the others would probably be dead, although, I began to think that they had probably turned to drugs and ended up dead one way or another with the upbringing that they had endured. I had not yet made my mind up on whether or not I felt sorry for Ian if he turned out to be the murderer, because although what the murderer did was beyond evil, their evil would have been forced upon them, although some would not have seen it like that. Some would have wanted justice for the people who suffered such awful deaths, and I did, in a way, because it was still unforgivable, despite the horrific upbringing Ian suffered. I just knew that evil does not appear: it has to come from somewhere.

I turned on the computer to do some research. Firstly, I discovered each of the names of the family members by looking for birth records, including Ian's. Ian was born in 1966, making him forty-six now, and when the first murder was committed in 1988, he would have been twenty-two years old, which, unsurprisingly, was similar to the age when serial killers first started killing, on average.

Now that I had the names, I needed to find out which ones were dead, which turned out to be most of them, except for Ernest Glow. Ernest had changed his name, and he was now untraceable. He got out while he could, I thought, leaving his brother to suffer alone with the monsters he lived with every day of his life with. Ernest just wanted to forget everything.

Hannah, the sister, had committed suicide; she took tablets and left a note, saying how much she hated the world and how glad she was to be finally out of it. Perhaps Ernest leaving the family gave Ian the motive to kill him, I thought.

The other family members also died in intriguing ways. Both of the grandparents had died in their homes on the same day. The autopsy report said that it was just a coincidence, that they had both died of old age, but it was still unusual. Trevor, the father, had died of cardiac arrest, aged fifty-six. Iris, the mother, had died of liver failure due to her alcoholism. The aunt had died in a fire, due to smoke inhalation, and the uncle died in a car crash, aged twenty-eight. I did not know why, but all of these deaths seemed to be more than coincidental. I thought it strange that four members of the same family would die of unnatural deaths; or even five, if Iris was to be included. Maybe Ian had murdered some of them himself, and discovered that he enjoyed watching them suffer, so he would want to repeat it again?

I knew that enough was enough: I was ready to arrest Ian for the murders, but I was not going to charge him yet, as I was almost too suspicious of him. I swore an oath to myself before entering the job: never assume anything unless there is concrete evidence to support it. I just needed to gather more evidence against him until I charged him, but I knew that I did not have much time.

At the end of the day, after having not made much progress in the case, I left the station for the night. As I walked out of the doors, I received a phone call. I looked, and it said it was Danny, my ex-fiancé. I cancelled the call. I was sick of him making these phone calls, and if he did not stop soon, I was going to arrest him for harassment. I had made it perfectly clear to him that I wanted nothing to do with him ever again; he made his bed, and now he had to sleep in it. He broke my heart, and nothing was ever going to change that.

Although my life was quite busy at the moment, I wanted to try and find space for somebody in my life. I had always been a loner. At school, I had one boyfriend for about three weeks. Nobody ever really liked me, and I didn't know why. I knew that I was not the ugliest of people, it was probably because I was too focused on my work. Throughout my school life, I pushed boys aside, and that was what got me here today. But now, I was determined that one day, I would find the one. I knew I would eventually, no matter how long it took.

After that depressing moment, I decided to forget about it and move on with my life. I went home, and looked at the notes and information about the case so far.

Chapter 9

I returned to the station the next day, thinking that it would be business as usual. In fact, I was about to get another lead in the case, because a relative of one of the victims said that they wanted to speak to me, with new information that I had not heard before. I was excited to see what it was, to see if it got me anywhere, and most importantly, to see if it gave me any more evidence to convict Ian Glow of the murders.

"Hello," said the woman, who appeared to be in her late sixties.

"What can I do for you?" I asked her, as politely as possible, just to show that the case of her relative was in good hands.

"Well," said the timid woman, "I am...was the daughter of Fred Aylesbury."

"That's right," I said, showing her that I had at least thought about her father, "he was the elderly man."

"Yes," she said, nervous. "Anyway, the news said that you have arrested Ian Glow. I came in as soon as I could."

"Yes," I replied, beginning to get excited with the thought that it might lead somewhere.

The woman continued. "Well, I think I have more evidence to help convict him, if he is guilty."

I almost jumped up with enthusiasm. Hopefully, this woman was correct, and that Ian Glow had slipped up somewhere.

"Please, tell me," I replied.

"Well," she said, "I don't know where else to start, but the beginning."

"And that is a very appropriate place to start," I said, trying to be as reassuring in my voice as possible, whilst pushing her to tell me about this evidence as quickly as she could.

"Well, it started a few months before my father was killed. I was coming to see him one day, and when I left, it was getting dark, so I got the fright of my life when I saw Ian Glow outside my dad's window!" she cried.

"Really?" I said, glad that my hopes were correct.

"Yes. Me and my sister got the fright of our lives. We asked him what he was doing and he just said, 'Sorry. I was looking for something'. But that wasn't the first time we had seen him there. We've seen him twice after that, me and one of my brothers, and then we think we saw him a few times after that, peering into my father's window."

"But you can't say for certain that it was him the last few times?"

"No, because it was dark, but we can only assume that it was him. He must be a head case anyway. Why would he peer into an old man's window like that?"

"Well, hopefully, I'll find that out for you," I replied, "but the only explanation I can give you right now is that Mr. Glow has problems."

"Well, does that help?" the elderly lady asked.

"Yes, it does actually," I said, "it helps a lot."

I was now more confident with the case; I was more confident that Ian Glow was indeed the killer I was searching for.

Then, suddenly, something came to me. Elizabeth Beckett, the elderly woman, was murdered with an axe, and not everybody buys axes these days! Even the type of axe was identified, so if I found a record of purchase for that specific axe, I would be able to find more evidence that pointed towards Ian Glow, because the person who bought the axe would have had to have shown an ID. There was a chance (no matter how small it was) that Ian Glow could show up on a record if the shopkeeper had bothered to write down the names.

My blood pulsed through my veins—I knew that something good was coming. Was this the breakthrough in the case I searched for. After an hour of looking for shops that sold that specific type of axe, I was fortunate enough to be able to trace one shop in the area that carried that type of axe, and it was the only shop that sold that type of axe available at that time in Manchester. I was so pleased with the results, but I knew that the search was not yet over.

I arrived at the shop, which was still there. To my luck, it was actually the same shopkeeper, who had worked there for over twenty years. I showed him the badge, and he seemed willing to help.

"I know you might find this strange, but I am investigating a cold case killing," I told him.

"Let me guess," said the shopkeeper, "are you the one investigating the killings that were on the television?"

"Yes...how did you know that?" I asked, intrigued.

"Just a guess," said the shopkeeper. "So, what can I do for you?"

"Well," I said, trying not to laugh with embarrassment, "I am investigating a murder that happened over twenty years ago, and I have recently discovered that the killer purchased an axe from this shop before they killed the victim."

The man looked shocked. "You mean he came here?" he said.

"Yes."

"And I've spoken to him?" he asked.

"Yes. I need to know if there are any records that show purchases in between the years of 1990 and 1991."

"As a matter of fact, there are," the man said, smiling. He went into another room for a minute, and came back out with a box. He then opened the box, and asked me what type of axe it was. I told him, and he responded.

"It looks like there are five people who bought this axe: Barry Scott, Melvin Sykes, Daniel Broughway, Harry Thudd and John Hughes."

I was devastated. Ian Glow was not mentioned in there. I checked the records myself, but there was still no Ian Glow. Without coming up with the possibility that the purchase was not actually recorded, I was more puzzled than anything.

"Is there a chance that the purchase might not be among these records?" I asked.

"I swear down on my son's life, I did not miss the purchase. I even had a sign up behind here to let them know that they were to receive a receipt, and before I gave them their receipt, I would write their names down in there. There is no possible way that I would miss it."

"Were you off work for one day at all?"

"I was at work every single day. I came here every Monday to Friday without fail."

"Were there any break-ins?" I said, desperate for an explanation to this.

"No. There has never been a break-in here either."

I sighed. "Well, if you think of anything, contact the police, please," I said to him.

"Actually, there is one thing," the man said.

"Oh, go on then," I asked, desperate for some more information.

"Well, just this one time, in about 1990, somebody acted a bit strange, and it made me very suspicious.

"He came up to me. He wore this sort of cowboy hat and sunglasses so I couldn't see his face. He was quite mysterious to start off with. Anyway, he put the axe down on the table, and he said, 'How much?'

"'That's £50.00', I replied, 'but you can get a cheaper one over there. That's pretty much the same one, but for £35.00'.

"He ran his fingers down the blade. 'I like this one', he said. He then pulled out £50.00 and handed it to me and I recorded his details and things.

"'You chop a lot of wood?' I had asked him.

"'No', he told me. That's what made me really suspicious. What else could you use an axe for, except chopping wood?"

"Did you get a name?" I asked him, hoping and praying that he would say yes.

"No," he replied, "I'm really sorry. I just can't remember, but it might have been one of these five." He pointed to the record book.

"Did you not think of reporting him to the police?"

"Why would I?" he replied, "I didn't think he was going to go and chop somebody up."

"Then what did you think?"

"I didn't know what to think, but it wasn't right!"

That shopkeeper gave me some fantastic leads. Was that mysterious man at the shop the killer? It was strange that he wore a sunhat and sunglasses indoors, too. For whatever reason, he did not want to be seen, and perhaps that was because he did not want to be identified. This killer is clever, I thought to myself, but hopefully, not as clever as me.

I returned to the station, intending to work on the information given to me, but I was astounded when a relative of another victim approached me. This must be my lucky day, I thought.

This time it was a young woman.

"I need to speak to you about my mother, Irene Dunneford," she said.

"OK," I said, hoping to get more information to make sense out of this whole thing, "we can sit down in the soft interview room."

We got sat down, and drinks were sorted.

"So, what is it you want to tell me?" I asked her.

"Well, I have some information which might or might not help you," she said.

"OK," I said, ready with my pen and notebook as ever.

"Well this one time, when I was nine, a couple of days before my mother died, my mother was driving me along in the car, through the woods part of town, and she was pulled over by a police car."

"A police car?"

"Yes. It was a dark night, and a policeman got out. I could hardly see him. I know that he was wearing a sunhat and sunglasses, which was very strange. Well, he said to my mother, 'Hello, missy.'

"'What do you want?' my mother said.

"'Well, I think you know the answer to that', he said.

"'I haven't been speeding, if that was what you're asking', she said.

"'You have', the man said, in a sort of cheeky tone of voice.

"'I haven't! I was going at thirty miles an hour!'

"'You know that's wrong', he said, 'so I need you to step out of the car'.

"'You're not even a policeman, are you?' she said.

"He laughed. 'Do you like hunting?' he said to her.

"'What are you talking about?' said my mother.

"'Because I do. Maybe we should go hunting some time'.

"My mother just drove off, distressed about what had happened."

"Did your mother report this man to the police?" I asked, learning more and more information about the potential killer.

"She did, but nothing was done about it. About four days later, my mother went missing."

This was extraordinary. I now had people who had seen the killer. I assumed that it was the killer, anyway, and it might have been the same man. It also might have been Ian Glow. I hoped that I could work from there, but I did not know where to go for now. I decided to go home, as usual, and see what tomorrow brought me.

Chapter 10

As a matter of fact, I received, yet, more information about the killer. This time, it was better, and bigger, than any previous information I had received. When I entered the station that day, a woman of about forty came up to me.

"Are you the one working on the serial killings case?" she said.

"I am," I replied, "and what can I do for you?"

"My name is Sally Juxton," she said, "and I have some information that might help you. Is there anywhere we can go?"

We sat down, and I eagerly asked Sally what she wanted to tell me about the killer.

"Well," Sally begun, "I was once kidnapped by a person who I think was the killer."

"What?!" I cried, expressing my shock and excitement at the same time. I had never thought that there could have been a survivor of this.

"This was in 1995. I remember it so clearly," she added.

"Please, tell me everything," I said, still in shock about what I had been told.

"Well, I was out one night, and I was quite drunk, so I got in one of those taxi things. You know, the ones that wait outside of clubs acting as taxis?"

I nodded, knowing how dangerous the people who drove them were.

"Anyway, I got in, and asked him to take me home. I was still quite drunk at the time. He started talking to me, asking me things like, 'do you like hunting?' and 'have you ever seen any horror films?' I thought it was strange but I didn't really think much else of it. Anyway, half an hour later, I was beginning to get worried, because it only took around twenty minutes to get home.

"By now, I was pretty much sobered up. I asked him where we were and he just said, 'you'll see'. He then laughed and told me I was going to die tonight. I was in shock. I tried to open the doors but they were child locked. I tried to scratch away at his face, but it didn't stop him. Suddenly, we were out in the middle of nowhere, and he dragged me out of the car. He told me to stay where I was or he was gonna shoot me there and then.

"I couldn't see anyone. I don't think we were even on a road. There were no cars, or buildings. He then told me we were going to play a little game. It was called run away from the killer or something like that.

Anyway, he got a chainsaw out of his boot, and then turned it on. I was terrified. I started to run, but he just chased me through the fields, laughing like a maniac. I eventually got into the woods without him catching me. I decided to hide in a bush somewhere for the time being. After about five minutes, I heard his footsteps again, and he was whispering, 'I'm coming to get you, Hannah. Oh, Hannah? You're not going to get away'

"It all went quiet, I tried not to breathe. Then, he revved up his chainsaw again and I just ran for it. I ran and ran. It must have been longer than an hour. I eventually got into the field again where I started. I was shocked when I saw a whole in the ground. I was beginning to think he'd dug a grave for me or something. I somehow managed to get on to a road without him finding me. It must have took two hours before I found help. By then, he was gone."

I just sat back, astonished by the horrific encounter that Sally had just recalled to me. I felt so sorry for her.

"Do you think it's the same killer?" she said.

"It looks that way," I replied.

"Could you do one thing for me?" Sally asked.

"What's that?"

"If you do ever find this person, could you come and tell me about him? I just want closure."

"I will," I replied, "but there are a couple of questions I need to ask you. Did you actually see what he looked like?"

The inevitable answer was no, and I knew that she was going to say that anyway. He had covered his face up with a hat and glasses. She told me she remembered him as quite broad, but that was it.

"Did you note what car it was? Did you get the license plate?" I asked her, knowing what the answer to those questions would be too.

"I wish I did," replied Sally, "and we could have nailed him."

"Don't worry," I said, "I won't give up until I find out who it is!"

"Do you have an idea?"

"We have somebody in custody, but I now think that it might not be him."

I was so confused. At the time, Sally would have been a young girl, so the killer had imagined her as Hannah Glow, Ian's sister. That was the evidence I needed. I now had proof that the killer was imagining killing somebody named "Hannah," and probably did the same for the rest. I knew it was probably Ian Glow, but there was still one other person I had in mind.

Shortly after Sally left, the boss told me that he had found out about a person who lives near the field where the bodies were found. He had telephoned the man who lived there, and he said that he would be willing to speak to me; so, my next stop was that house.

The house was actually half a mile away from the field where the bodies were dug up, but that was the nearest building to it. The inhabitant of the house, Thomas Baker, had lived there for almost all of his life, so he might have seen something all of those years ago.

I knocked on the door, and he invited me in. I got straight to the point. To my pleasant surprise, Thomas had seen something. He described one night in the late 1980s, where he saw a mysterious figure, presumably a man, walking through the back fields of his house, wielding a sharp knife. He wore very large goggles and a gun shield. He also wore a helmet. Earlier in the night, Thomas thought he had heard a scream, but he could not be certain. He asked him what he was doing, all dressed like that, but the man just glared at him and moved on.

I returned to the station, thinking about what Thomas had told me. It was fairly clear that the person Thomas described was the killer. However, why would he be wearing large goggles and a gun shield? I ran those two things through my head several times.

Goggles. Gun shield. Goggles. Gun shield.

Suddenly, it came to me. I did not solve the case completely yet, but I knew that I was way further forward. Something that somebody had said to me earlier just came to me, and it strongly linked with one of the items described. Could this solve the case? I hoped it would.

Chapter 11

The thing that I realized was that Yvonne Lennox, the first victim, carried pepper spray due to her attack. So, before killing Yvonne Lennox, the killer wore goggles to protect himself from the pepper spray attack, leaving Yvonne defenseless.

However, that did not answer the question of how the killer knew that she carried pepper spray, nor did it answer why the he wore a gun shield. I decided to look further to see if somebody who was murdered by this maniac was convicted of carrying a gun. As a matter of fact, one of the male victims, John Christie, was convicted of accidentally shooting somebody for hunting in the woods! This showed that he carried a gun around, which explained why the killer wore a gun shield, but how did he know?

Suddenly, it came to me. The only possible explanation for this was that the killer had read the police reports—it was the only possible way of finding out. I became thrilled as I realized that the only people who could have access to those files were the very people working in this station. I told the boss.

"Oh my God!" he cried, as if he had seen a ghost.

"What is it?" I asked, surprised at his reaction to the fantastic news.

"The only person who had access to those files— the only person who handled those files back then was Barry Scott."

"Who was he?" I asked.

"He's still here. He's a police officer now, but he used to handle files here years ago. I used to be acquainted with him, but now, we don't really speak since we're in different parts of the station." The boss was still in shock. "Do you think it could be true?" he said to me.

"It looks that way," I said, "because how else could the killer know what to wear for each person?"

"I know," said Mitchell, putting his hands in his head. "Don't arrest him yet, though, because there is not enough evidence. It's only assumptions."

"I know," I said, trying not to get over excited.

Just then, I remembered something else: in the list of people who bought an axe in between the years of 1990 and 1991, Barry Scott was on that list! Could this really be happening? Did we finally have him?

Obviously, that meant that the killer was not Ian Glow if it turned out to be this man, but there was another possibility: Ernest Glow. Since he was not called that any more, I did some research into Barry's background to see if he was born Barry. Mitchell gave me all of the details, and I typed them up into the computer for a birth record. Could Ernest be the real killer?

After a couple of minutes, that theory was disproven, since I had found a valid birth record for Barry Scott, so Barry Scott was not born Ernest Glow. Ernest had just disappeared.

"So, we still can't make an arrest?" I asked Mitchell, trying to think of a reason why this police officer would kill random people.

"No," Mitchell replied, "there is still not enough evidence. There is no DNA to link him to the murders, so we, or you, need to get a confession out of him."

I knew that there was a lot on the line here. If I did not manage to get a confession out of him, that would mean justice would not be brought to eight families (or at least eight, there could have been more that we did not know about). I was frightened.

When I saw this man, however, I was astounded that I had seen him before, during this investigation: he was the police officer who brought Ian Glow in, claiming that he had found him in the field. Now, I was convinced that it was him.

Barry, who lived near the Glow family, obviously liked to kill people, for whatever reason. Perhaps he was psychologically damaged himself due to physical or sexual abuse. He was also a very intelligent man, since when he started killing, he chose a deserted spot so that nobody would hear him. However, he deliberately left clues in order to frame Ian Glow: every murder victim looked like one family member, except for Ian. The survivor claimed that the killer was saying 'Hannah', Ian's big sister, and Ian was lurking around the field where the bodies were found. He only said the name of Ian's big sister so that in the future, it would point to Ian Glow, should the bodies ever be found. However, he was not as smart as he thought, because there were gaps, gaps that led us to him, and now, he was about to get caught out; at least, I hoped he did.

Mitchell sat him down in a room, and tried to keep him calm, by suggesting it was only a talk, and he was free to leave the room at any time. Meanwhile, I stared through the glass at him, and Miranda approached me saying, "It's definitely him. One hundred percent."

"I know," I replied, satisfied now that this man was indeed the killer I was searching for.

Mitchell left the room, leaving Barry on his own to wait. Barry lifted his head and looked at the mirror, knowing we were behind it, watching him. He grinned. Apprehension tickled over my skin as I realized that I was dealing with a complete and utter psychopath.

Chapter 12

I really had no idea how to approach this "talk"; this man was very intelligent, so it would take a lot to make him confess. He must have known that we were on to him, and that was what made me scared. I just took a deep breath, and entered the room.

"Hello, Tammy," he said, in a plain tone of voice.

"Hello, Barry," I replied, echoing his tone.

"Before we proceed," Barry began, "I just want to remind you that I can leave this room at any time. This is just a talk, right?"

"Right," I replied, trying not to stress him out.

"So, what do you want to talk about?" he said, sitting back, with his arms over the chair.

I knew he had it all planned out. He knew exactly what he was going to say; he'd had this day planned for years.

"I want to talk about the serial killings, Barry," I said, "and I'm trying to create a profile of the killer to discover his motives behind the killings."

"Well, I can give you a little information," he said, with a smirk. "I can give you my thoughts and views about what a serial killer thinks like. Although, I don't know myself, because I am not one myself." He paused and looked at me, "I've come across a lot of maniacs in my time, being in the police force."

"So, then," I said, interested in what he had to say, "what does the murderer enjoy about killing people?"

"He likes to see people suffer," Barry replied, "and he likes to be in control. He likes to hear the begging, and the desperation."

"So why does he kill them?"

"Oh, there could be many reasons. Perhaps he just gets a buzz out of killing people. It might be a sexual desire, but in some cases, he might be imagining killing someone else."

I paused for a second. I hated this man so much.

"So," I said, "why does he choose people with families?"

"It makes them more desperate to escape; they fight more because they know they have a reason to live, even the old ones."

"And why murder a child?"

"Because he wants to see how a child would react. Children think and act differently than adults." He laughed a little.

Inside I felt sick. All the while, he gave little hints to me that he was the killer, as though taunting me.

"So, what your trying to say is, the killer chooses a variety of people because he likes to choose a variety of ways. They would get bored if they just kill one type of person all the time?"

"That's what I'm saying," he said, "and it looks like the killer in this was like that."

I decided to put more pressure on him.

"So, how does it explain how the killer knew to wear protection from certain individuals?"

"That's where you're off track," he laughed, "I've heard about your investigation into this," he said, "and you did not pick up on the fact that the killer wore both the gun shield and the goggles at the same time."

"And?"

"Well, if the killer was killing the person who carried pepper spray, why would they choose to wear the gun shield? And vice versa."

I stopped for a second. Barry was right.

"Perhaps the killer just likes to wear those for every person, just in case they did actually escape, so they would not be able to be identified later. You're not so clever now, are you?" he laughed.

I felt ashamed. I got it wrong! I knew I had to move on.

"So, you like reading?" I asked him.

"I love it," he replied.

"What kind of books do you read?"

"Well, I like to read a variety of books. What about you? Don't tell me! I can guess!"

"Go on then."

"Well, you like to read detective stories. You're completely obsessed with them, aren't you?"

"Where did you get that idea from?" I cried, insulted.

"I can just imagine you now, sitting in your house on a Sunday afternoon, digging into those Agatha Christie books."

As a matter of fact, I did like to read detective stories; this man could read me as well.

"Let's move on," I said, determined to catch him.

"What is there to talk about now?" asked Barry, grinning.

"Let's talk about why you bought that axe!" I cried.

"Ha!" he yelled, "you're not going to catch me out there, Tammy!"

"What do you mean by that?" I asked him.

"Once again, you are going in the wrong direction."

"I'll have you know I've solved every murder I've investigated!"

"And how many is that?" he said, "excluding the gang killings, which are easy! Well, let's see, there was the Anne Le Trevell case, the Rupert Christen case, and recently, those serial killings from the other week. Congratulations! What a fantastic, world-class detective!" he laughed. "Do you really believe that you can solve any murder that's thrown at you?"

"Maybe," I said.

"Wake up, Tammy!" he cried. "Every detective has at least one murder that they don't solve! Probably more!"

"Well, I'll cross that bridge when I come to it," I said, "and anyway, I see you've done your homework on me."

He smiled and nodded his head.

"There was one more murder I forgot to mention." He stood up and put his lips next to my ear. "Your grandmother's."

"And I solved that, too!"

"Well, it could have been prevented!"

"No, it couldn't have!"

"Yes, it could! If you discovered that diary before she was killed, she might still be here today."

"Nice try, Barry," I said, "but you can't get to me."

"I am," he laughed, "and now that the person who killed your grandmother is dead, you feel that justice was not properly served. She only died a few months after going to jail for it, so you feel that she should have suffered for much longer after making your grandmother's life Hell."

"You still aren't getting to me," I said, defenseless.

"Just think about the way she was killed, Tammy. That knife went into her, oh, seven times? That's the usual amount of stab wounds a killer applies to their victim."

I tried to hold back the tears, and just about succeeded, but I knew that he saw them.

"You've never gotten over her murder, have you?" he whispered.

"Well," I said, "I've done my homework on you, as well!" she cried.

Barry's face turned upside down.

"So, you were turned down for being a security guard in a supermarket, failed the physical for being a fireman, and oh, this is the best one: failed the test to become an ambulance driver!"

I gave out a hysterical laugh, while Barry glared at me.

"Is that why you killed all those people, Barry?" I asked him, "because you resent the public?"

Barry's pinched face could have frozen vinegar. "That might be why he killed those people."

"No, Barry, let's face it. It was you who killed those people! I know it; you know it; and the rest of the team watching us knows it!"

Barry faced the door. "I'm done talking," he said.

At that point, I felt desperate.

"No, you're not," I said to him.

"Yes, I am," he said, opening the door and walking out.

I followed him out of the room. Barry turned around, and said to me, "Do you like hunting?"

"No, I don't," I replied.

"Well, you should try it. I might take you one day."

I smiled, and turned to the rest of the team, letting him walk out of the building because there was no evidence to convict him.

"That's it, isn't it?" I said, with tears in my eyes.

"I can only assure you that justice will be done one day," said DI Hobsworth.

"How?" I said, crying now. "How is he going to get caught out?"

There was no reply to that. I knew that he had gotten away with murder. It was the first case where I had not brought justice to the victims, nor their relatives.

I walked over to the investigation board, where it contained photographs of all eight victims. One by one, I pulled the photos down from there, knowing that nothing had changed for any of their family members. Those photos haunted me as I pulled them from the wall and stuck them into a cold case box. Although the families knew the truth about their loved ones' disappearance, the most important part had not been sorted out.

I was almost sick. When I left work that day, I decided that I needed a drink. I entered a local pub and stopped. Barry was there, laughing with friends, and one even offered to buy him a drink. He looked at me for a second, but then went back to his socializing. He was living a good life, and I could have stopped it. They asked for my story and I have told it. Enough.

About the Author

Brie Krauss lives in the United States with her family. Though not planning on becoming a writer, she had a few murder mysteries rolling around in her head and decided to write them on day, mostly so she could stop thinking about them. Always a fan of novellas, and quick entertainment, she kept the Closed Case stories short on purpose and hopes you enjoy them.

More by Brie Kraus

Closed case

Curious Confession
Murder on the Eiffel Tower
Over The Hills

Other Books

Don't Ask
I Hate You Rock Stars

.

www.ingramcontent.com/pod-product-compliance
Lightning Source LLC
Chambersburg PA
CBHW050834180626

46814CB00004B/1613